Little Red Riding Hood

Once upon a time there was a small girl called Little Red Riding Hood. She lived with her parents beside a deep, dark forest.

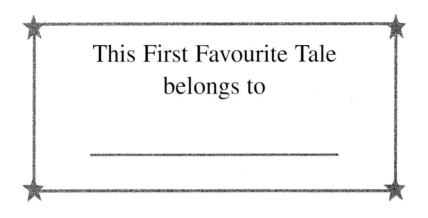

This First Favourite Tale
belongs to

BASED ON THE STORY BY JACOB AND WILHELM GRIMM

retold by Mandy Ross ★ *illustrated by* Anja Rieger

Published by Ladybird Books Ltd
A Penguin Company
Penguin Books Ltd, 80 Strand, London WC2R 0RL, UK
Penguin Books Australia Ltd, Camberwell, Victoria, Australia
Penguin Books (NZ) Ltd, Private Bag, 102902, NSMC, Auckland 10, New Zealand

19 20

© LADYBIRD BOOKS MCMXCIX

ISBN-13: 978-0-72149-734-1
ISBN-10: 0-7214-9734-9

Printed in Italy

…a big, bad wolf.

"Grandmother's poorly," said Little Red Riding Hood's mother one day. "Please take her this cake. But don't stop on the way!"

So Little Red Riding Hood set off through the deep, dark forest. She looked all around.

There wasn't a sound.

Then who should she meet but…

…the big, bad wolf.

"Good day, my dear," growled the wolf with a big, bad smile. "What are you doing here?"

The wolf had a plan.

"Wouldn't your grandmother like some of these flowers?" he smiled.

"What a good idea," said Little Red Riding Hood. And she stopped to pick a big bunch.

Meanwhile, the wolf sped ahead through
the deep, dark forest. At last he arrived at…

…Grandmother's cottage.

"I'm HUNGRY," thought the big, bad wolf, licking his lips. And he knock-knock-knocked at the door.

"Hello, Grandmother," growled the wolf. "It's Little Red Riding Hood."

"That sounds more like the big, bad wolf," thought Grandmother, and she crept quickly under the bed.

The wolf went in. He looked all around, but there wasn't a sound.

Then his tummy rumbled.

"No one's here," he grumbled. "Never mind.
Little Red Riding Hood will be along soon."

It's dusty! I
mustn't sneeze.

Quickly the wolf put on Grandmother's dressing gown and nightcap. Then he hopped into bed and pretended to nap.

"Heh! Heh! Heh!" he snarled. "Little Red Riding Hood will never know it's me!"

Soon Little Red Riding Hood knock-knock-knocked at the door.

"Hello, Grandmother," she called.
"It's Little Red Riding Hood."

"Come in, my dear," growled the wolf.

Little Red Riding Hood opened the door.

"Oh, Grandmother!" she gasped…

"…What big ears you have!"

"All the better to hear you with, my dear," growled the wolf.

"And Grandmother, what big eyes you have!"

"All the better to see you with, my dear," growled the wolf.

"And Grandmother, what big teeth you have!"

"All the better to…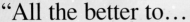

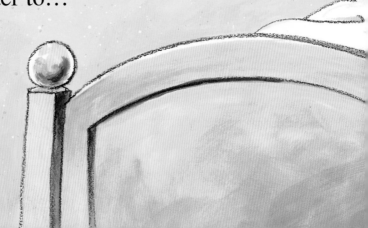

"...GOBBLE YOU UP!" roared the wolf.

But as he leapt out of bed, Grandmother's nightcap flopped right over his head.

"Quick! Down here, dear!" whispered
Grandmother, and she pulled Little Red
Riding Hood under the bed.

Just then, a woodcutter passed by the cottage.
He heard a growling and howling...

and he dashed inside.
With one *SWISH!* of his axe he killed
the big, bad wolf.

The woodcutter looked all around. But there wasn't a sound. And then…

...out crept Little Red Riding Hood and Grandmother from under the bed.

And Little Red Riding Hood said,
"Mother was right. I'll *never* stop again
on my way through the forest!"